MINDFUL
ABCs

Written & Illustrated by Tamara Hackett

Sweet Clover Studios

Published by: Sweet Clover Studios

Author & Illustrator: Tamara Hackett

ISBN : 978-0-9948875-0-4

For more by Sweet Clover Studios please visit:

www.sweetcloverstudios.com or

www.tamarahackett.com

Special Thanks to Mindfulness Teacher Lyndsey Burton from www.lyndseyburton.co.uk
Disclaimer: This book and its contents are not meant as a substitute for a dictionary or an absolute

governing definition. Upon reading this book to your children (or for yourself), the author disclaims

liability for the use or interpretation of the information. Zimzum is also a term used by Rob and Kristen

Bell but is not associated with their teachings and work.

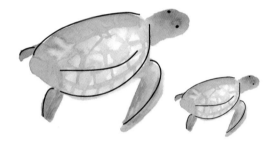

dedicated to my little ones

Mindful ABCs is meant to be an easy introduction
to vocabulary and concepts that can support the overall well-being
and 'awareness of feelings' in a little one's life.

By writing this book and sharing these personal definitions, I am hoping to encourage conversations
about these words and increase appreciation of how they show up in our everyday lives.

On each page you will see a capital letter of the alphabet followed by a
definition (as perceived and shared by me), as well as an illustration of an animal.
With my many years of experience with children, I have found that having something
to 'look' for/at on each page is another point of engagement and interest.
It is also an easy and familiar point of reference to start a chat about if the
'new' words are taking a while to sink in.

The illustrations are also meant to introduce children to a different design aesthetic. Feel free to let them guess what animal is on each page or what else they see in the design.

I also suggest a light-hearted approach to this book, not stressing any concepts in particular. Children learn through repetition and experience. So the most important thing is making the time spent reading an enjoyable and positive experience. So...

ENJOY!

IS FOR **APPRECIATION**

A is for *appreciation*

Appreciation is a way to show your excitement and thankfulness. For everything you have and all that you experience.

(...and for ANT)

IS FOR BELIEF

B is for *belief*

Belief is when you know something in your heart is true.

(...and for BUTTERFLY)

IS FOR CREATE

C is for *create*

Creating is a process of using your wonderful skills
to make something that wasn't there before.

(...and for COW)

IS FOR **DREAMS**

D is for *dreams*

Dreams are wishes that you hold in your heart.

(...and for DRAGONFLY)

IS FOR **ENERGY**

E is for *energy*

When you have energy you feel a powerful excitement,
inside and out.

(...and for ELEPHANT)

IS FOR **FREEDOM**

F is for *freedom*

Freedom is a feeling that anything can happen and nothing is in your way.

(...and for FROG)

IS FOR **GRATEFUL**

G is for *grateful*

Grateful is like appreciation. It's a filled up feeling that makes you notice all of the great things in your life.

(...and for GIRAFFE)

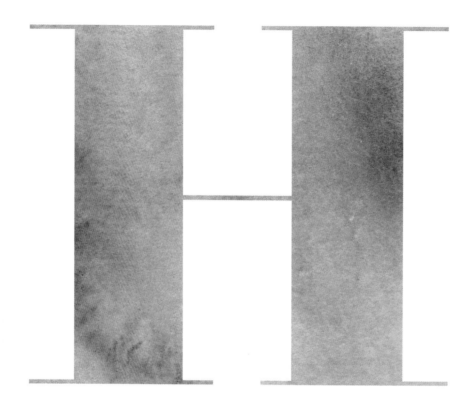

IS FOR **HAPPINESS**

H is for *happiness*

Happiness is a feeling that makes you smile and act on your good thoughts.

(...and for HIPPO)

IS FOR INSPIRATION

I is for *inspiration*

Inspiration is when something stirs an *inside* feeling to do something good.

(...and for INCHWORM)

IS FOR **JOY**

J is for *joy*

Joy is allowing excitement to fill you up and appear as smiles, giggles and laughs.

(...and for JELLYFISH)

IS FOR **KNOWING**

K is for *knowing*

Knowing is a strong, positive feeling inside of you that
will help you decide what to do.

(...and for KOALA BEAR)

IS FOR **LOVE**

L is for *love*

Love is everything. All the wonderful feelings in your life,
mixed together then shown to the world.

(...and for LADYBUG)

IS FOR MINDFUL

M is for *mindful*

Being mindful is listening to all your senses to learn about your mind, body and the world around you.

(...and for MOOSE)

IS FOR NATURE

N is for *nature*

Nature is the world's gifts to us. The outdoors and all of its beauty.

(...and for NEWT)

IS FOR OPEN

O is for open

Open is how you can act and feel when you want to learn something, remember and let new ideas into your mind.

(...and for OCTOPUS)

IS FOR **PRESENCE**

P is for *presence*

Presence is keeping your thoughts on the people and things that are with you in that moment.

(...and for PIG)

IS FOR QUIET

Q is for *quiet*

Quiet is when you don't hear sounds and your mind feels calm.

(...and for QUAIL)

IS FOR **RELEASE**

R is for *release*

Release is a way of letting go. You can release a thought
and think about something new.

(...and for RHINOCEROS)

IS FOR SENSES

S is for *senses*

Your senses help you understand yourself and others by noticing what you see, feel, smell, touch and taste.

(...and for SNAKE)

IS FOR **THOUGHTS**

T is for *thoughts*

Thoughts are the quiet words and feelings in your mind
that you don't always say out loud.

(...and for TURTLE)

IS FOR **UNLIMITED**

U is for *unlimited*

Unlimited is when you feel like nothing
can hold you back.

(...and for URCHIN)

IS FOR **VOICE**

V is for *voice*

Using your voice is a way to express what you feel and think with your words.

(...and for VULTURE)

IS FOR WONDERFUL

W is for *wonderful*

Wonderful is a way to say how amazing something is.

(...and for WHALE)

IS FOR EXPLORE

X is for *eXplore*

Exploring is a way of finding out more about yourself
and the world around you.

(...and for X-RAY FISH)

IS FOR **YOGA**

Y is for *yoga*

Yoga is a way to connect your breath,
thoughts and body.

(...and for YAK)

IS FOR ZIMZUM

Z is for *zimzum*

Zimzum is a way to notice and appreciate the love between two people.

(...and for ZEBRA)

Made in the USA
Charleston, SC
24 November 2015